PUFFIN BOOKS

MORE STORIES FOR UNDER-FIVES

Here is another collection of magical stories which have been chosen especially for reading aloud to children. The Corrins have selected a marvellously rich variety of stories to capture the imagination. They range from the ever-popular 'Teddy Robinson' and 'My Naughty Little Sister' to the surprising tale of how Fear-No-Bear got his name and the mystery of Mr Hak-Tak's big brass cooking pot. There's the story of the little girl who gets out of bed on the wrong side and the cat who gets bigger and bigger . . . and bigger. All the stories are touched with magic and humour and will soon become firm favourites!

Sara and Stephen Corrin are editors of many popular anthologies for children. Sara was born within the sound of Bow Bells and has all the cockney's good humour and jaunty repartee. She travels considerably, telling stories, especially in children's libraries, and has made the subject of children's responses to literature one of her main studies. Stephen Corrin was brought up on a mixed diet of the *Gem*, the *Magnet*, the Bible, cricket and Beethoven quartets. He reviews, writes stories and translates from French, Russian, German and Danish.

GW00725920

Other collections
from Sara and Stephen Corrin

More Stories for Under-Fives

Sara and
Stephen Corrin

Illustrated by
Vanessa Julian-Ottie

PUFFIN BOOKS

PUFFIN BOOKS

Published by the Penguin Group
27 Wrights Lane, London w8 5tz, England
Viking Penguin Inc., 40 West 23rd Street, New York, New York 10010, USA
Penguin Books Australia Ltd, Ringwood, Victoria, Australia
Penguin Books Canada Ltd, 2801 John Street, Markham, Ontario, Canada l3r 1b4
Penguin Books (NZ) Ltd, 182–190 Wairau Road, Auckland 10, New Zealand

Penguin Books Ltd, Registered Offices: Harmondsworth, Middlesex, England

This selection published by Faber and Faber 1988
Published in Puffin Books 1988
1 3 5 7 9 10 8 6 4 2

Made and printed in Great Britain by
Richard Clay Ltd, Bungay, Suffolk

Contents

Contents

Acknowledgements

We are grateful to the under-mentioned authors, publishers and agents for permission to include the following:

'The Baker's Cat' from *A Necklace of Raindrops* by Joan Aiken, published by Jonathan Cape Ltd.

'My Naughty Little Sister and the Workmen' from *My Naughty Little Sister* by Dorothy Edwards, published by Methuen Children's Books.

'The Elephant and the Bad Baby' by Elfrida Vipont, published by Hamish Hamilton Ltd.

'Fear-No-Bear' by Dick King-Smith, © Dick King-Smith 1986.

'Two of Everything' from *The Treasure of Li-Po* by Alice Ritchie, published by The Bodley Head.

'The Giraffe who Saw to the End of the World' from *The Elephant and the Flower* by Brian Patten, published by Allen and Unwin.

'The Little Red Engine Gets a Name' by Diana Ross, reprinted by permission of Mrs Teresa Anderson.

'The Little Girl who Got Out of Bed the Wrong Side' from *Three Bags Full* by Ruth Ainsworth. © Ruth Ainsworth 1972, 1975. Reprinted by permission of William Heinemann Ltd.

'My Puppy' by Aileen Fisher, by permission of the author.

'Brown Bear on a Brown Chair' by Irina Hale, reprinted by permission of Macmillan.

'The Leopard that Lost a Spot' from *The Anita Hewett Animal Story Book* by Anita Hewett, published by The Bodley Head.

'The Girl and the Crocodile' from *Tales for Telling* by Leila Berg, published by Methuen Children's Books.

'The Magic Umbrella' by Rose Fyleman, reprinted by permission of the Society of Authors as the Literary Representative of the Estate of Rose Fyleman.

'Teddy Robinson Goes to the Toyshop' (in a shortened version) and 'Teddy Robinson is a Polar Bear' from *Dear Teddy Robinson* by Joan G. Robinson, published by Harrap.

Another Brief Word to the Story-teller

Choosing stories for this highly impressionable age-group is somewhat less than plain sailing. It demands a careful – even wary – understanding of growing children and the way they perceive and construct the big wide world.

We hope that the stories we have selected will help children to understand their everyday lives, while fostering their latent curiosity by showing them strange things happening and people behaving in ways unlike their own.

There is much in this collection for children to wonder at, as they listen, wide-eyed, to a variety of events, and get to know a rich gallery of colourful characters. There is also much, of course, to make them laugh with sheer enjoyment.

Around the age of four the child becomes fascinated with the idea of magic. Most of these tales will cast their own spell and we hope children will come to love them and want to hear them over and over again.

It matters little whether the heroes are animals, humans or machines; children will readily identify with any of them. The Little Red Engine, for example, is itself almost a child; it yearns to be important and respected and, after a series of adventures, succeeds in achieving this. In all the stories things go wrong and then come right.

Stories like these will, we feel sure, lead the child naturally on to the wider fields of imaginative literature.

The Baker's Cat

JOAN AIKEN

Once there was an old lady, Mrs Jones, who lived with her cat, Mog. Mrs Jones kept a baker's shop, in a little tiny town, at the bottom of a valley between two mountains.

Every morning you could see Mrs Jones's light twinkle on, long before all the other houses in the town, because she got up very early to bake loaves and buns and jam tarts and Welsh cakes.

First thing in the morning Mrs Jones lit a big fire. Then she made dough, out of flour and water and sugar and yeast. Then she put the dough into pans and set it in front of the fire to rise.

Mog got up early too. He got up to catch mice. When he had chased all the mice out of the bakery, he wanted to sit in front of the warm fire. But Mrs Jones wouldn't let him, because of the loaves and buns there, rising in their pans.

She said, 'Don't sit on the buns, Mog.'

The buns were rising nicely. They were getting fine and big. That is what yeast does. It makes bread and buns and cakes swell up and get bigger and bigger.

As Mog was not allowed to sit by the fire, he went to play in the sink.

Most cats hate water, but Mog didn't. He loved it. He liked to sit by the tap, hitting the drops with his paw as they fell, and getting water all over his whiskers!

What did Mog look like? His back, and his sides, and his legs down as far as where his socks would have come to, and his face and ears and his tail were all marmalade-coloured. His stomach and his waist-coat and his paws were white. And he had a white tassel at the tip of his tail, white fringes to his ears, and white whiskers. The water made his marmalade fur go almost fox-colour and his paws and waistcoat shining-white clean.

But Mrs Jones said, 'Mog, you are getting too excited. You are shaking water all over my pans of buns, just when they are getting nice and big. Run along and play outside.'

Mog was affronted. He put his ears and tail down (when cats are pleased they put their ears and tails up) and he went out. It was raining hard.

A rushing rocky river ran through the middle of the town. Mog went and sat in the water and looked for fish. But there were no fish in that part of the river. Mog got wetter and wetter. But he didn't care. Presently he began to sneeze.

Then Mrs Jones opened her door and called, 'Mog! I have put the buns in the oven. You can come in now, and sit by the fire.'

Mog was so wet that he was shiny all over, as if he had been polished. As he sat by the fire he sneezed nine times.

Mrs Jones said, 'Oh dear, Mog, are you catching a cold?'

She dried him with a towel and gave him some warm milk with yeast in it. Yeast is good for people when they are poorly.

Then she left him sitting in front of the fire and

began making jam tarts. When she had put the tarts in the oven she went out shopping, taking her umbrella.

But what do you think was happening to Mog?

The yeast was making him rise.

As he sat dozing in front of the lovely warm fire he was growing bigger and bigger.

First he grew as big as a sheep.

Then he grew as big as a donkey.

Then he grew as big as a cart-horse.

Then he grew as big as a hippopotamus.

By now he was too big for Mrs Jones's little kitchen, but he was far too big to get through the door. He just burst the walls.

When Mrs Jones came home with her shopping-bag and her umbrella she cried out,

'Mercy me, what is happening to my house?'

The whole house was bulging. It was swaying. Huge whiskers were poking out of the kitchen window. A marmalade-coloured paw came out of one bedroom window, and an ear with a white fringe out of the other.

'Morow?' said Mog. He was waking up from his nap and trying to stretch.

Then the whole house fell down.

'Oh, Mog!' cried Mrs Jones. 'Look what you've done.'

The people in the town were very astonished when they saw what had happened.

They gave Mrs Jones the Town Hall to live in, because they were so fond of her (and her buns). But they were not so sure about Mog.

The Mayor said, 'Suppose he goes on growing and

breaks our Town Hall? Suppose he turns fierce? It would not be safe to have him in the town, he is too big.'

Mrs Jones said, 'Mog is a gentle cat. He would not hurt anybody.'

'We will wait and see about that,' said the Mayor. 'Suppose he sat down on someone? Suppose he was hungry? What will he eat? He had better live outside the town, up on the mountain.'

So everybody shouted, 'Shoo! Scram! Pssst! Shoo!' and poor Mog was driven outside the town gates. It was still raining hard. Water was rushing down the mountains. Not that Mog cared.

But poor Mrs Jones was very sad. She began making a new lot of loaves and buns in the Town Hall, crying into them so much that the dough was too wet, and very salty.

Mog walked up the valley between the two mountains. By now he was bigger than an elephant – almost as big as a whale! When the sheep on the mountain saw him coming, they were scared to death and galloped away. But he took no notice of them. He was looking for fish in the river. He caught lots of fish! He was having a fine time.

By now it had been raining for so long that Mog heard a loud, watery roar at the top of the valley. He saw a huge wall of water coming towards him. The river was beginning to flood, as more and more rain-water poured down into it, off the mountains.

Mog thought, 'If I don't stop that water, all these

fine fish will be washed away.'

So he sat down, plump in the middle of the valley, and he spread himself out like a big, fat cottage loaf.

The water could not get by.

The people in the town had heard the roar of the flood-water. They were very frightened. The Mayor shouted, 'Run up the mountains before the water gets to the town, or we shall all be drowned!'

So they all rushed up the mountains, some on one side of the town, some on the other.

What did they see then?

Why, Mog sitting in the middle of the valley. Beyond him was a great lake.

'Mrs Jones,' said the Mayor, 'can you make your cat stay there till we have built a dam across the valley, to keep all that water back?'

'I will try,' said Mrs Jones. 'He mostly sits still if he is tickled under his chin.'

So for three days everybody in the town took turns

tickling Mog under his chin with hay-rakes. He purred and purred and purred. His purring made big waves roll right across the lake of flood-water.

All this time the best builders were making a great dam across the valley.

People brought Mog all sorts of nice things to eat, too – bowls of cream and condensed milk, liver and bacon, sardines, even chocolate! But he was not very hungry. He had eaten so much fish.

On the third day they finished the dam. The town was safe.

The Mayor said, 'I can see now that Mog is a gentle cat. He can live in the Town Hall with you, Mrs Jones. Here is a badge for him to wear.'

The badge was on a silver chain to go round his neck. It said MOG SAVED OUR TOWN.

So Mrs Jones and Mog lived happily ever after in the Town Hall. If you should go to the little town of Carnmog you may see the policeman holding up the traffic while Mog walks through the streets on his way to catch fish in the lake for breakfast. His tail waves above the houses and his whiskers rattle against the upstairs windows. But people know he will not hurt them, because he is a gentle cat.

He loves to play in the lake and sometimes he gets so wet that he sneezes. But Mrs Jones is not going to give him any more yeast.

He is quite big enough already!

My Naughty Little Sister
and the Workmen

DOROTHY EDWARDS

When my sister was a naughty little girl, she was very, very inquisitive. She was always looking and peeping into things that didn't belong to her. She used to open other people's cupboards and boxes just to find out what was inside.

Aren't you glad you're not inquisitive like that?

Well now, one day a lot of workmen came to dig up all the roads near our house, and my little sister was very interested in them. They were very nice men, but some of them had rather loud shouty voices sometimes. There were shovelling men, and picking men, and men with jumping-about things that went, 'ah-ah-ah-ah-ah-ah-aha-aaa,' and men who drank tea out of jam-pots, and men who cooked sausages over fires, and there was an old, old man who sat up all night when the other men had gone home, and who had a lot of coats and scarves to keep him warm.

There were lots of things for my little inquisitive sister to see, there were heaps of earth, and red lanterns for the old, old man to light at night time, and long poley things to keep the people from falling down the holes in the road, and workmen's huts, and many other things.

When the workmen were in our road, my little sister used to watch them every day. She used to lean over the gate and stare and stare, but when they went off to the next road she didn't see so much of them.

Well now, I will tell you about the inquisitive thing my little sister did one day, shall I?

Yes. Well, do you remember Bad Harry who was my little sister's best boy-friend? Now this Bad Harry came one day to ask my mother if my little sister could go round to his house to play with him, and as Bad Harry's house wasn't far away, and as there were no roads to cross, my mother said my little sister could go.

So my little sister put on her hat and her coat, and her scarf and her gloves, because it was a nasty cold day, and went off with her best boy-friend to play with him.

They hurried along like good children until they came to the workmen in the next road, and then they went slow as slow, because there were so many things to see. They looked at this, and at that, and when they got past the workmen they found a very curious thing.

By the road there was a tall hedge, and under the tall hedge there was a mackintoshy bundle.

Now this mackintoshy bundle hadn't anything to do with Bad Harry, and it hadn't anything to do with my naughty little sister, yet, do you know, they were so inquisitive they stopped and looked at it.

They had such a good look at it that they had to get right under the hedge to see, and when they got very near it they found it was an old mackintosh wrapped round something or other inside.

Weren't they naughty? They should have gone straight home to Bad Harry's mother's house, shouldn't they? But they didn't. They stayed and looked at the mackintoshy bundle.

And they opened it. They really did. It wasn't their bundle, but they opened it wide under the hedge, and do you know what was inside it? I know you aren't an inquisitive meddlesome child, but would you like to know?

Well, inside the bundle there were lots and lots of parcels and packages tied up in red handkerchiefs, and brown paper, and newspaper, and instead of putting them back again like nice children, those little horrors started to open all those parcels, and inside those parcels there were lots of things to eat!

There were sandwiches, and cakes, and meat pies, and cold cooked fish, and eggs, and goodness knows what-all.

Weren't those bad children surprised? They couldn't think how all those sandwiches and things could have got into that old mackintosh.

Then Bad Harry said, 'Shall we eat some?' You remember he was a greedy lad. But my little sister said, 'No, it's picked-up food.' My little sister knew that my mother had told her never, never to eat picked-up food. You see she was good about *that*.

Only she was very bad after, because she said, 'I know, let's play with it.'

So they took out all those sandwiches and cakes, and meat-pies and cold cooked fish and eggs, and they laid them out across the path and made them into pretty patterns on the ground. Then Bad Harry threw a sandwich at my little sister and she threw a meat-pie at him, and they began to have a lovely game.

And then do you know what happened? A big roary voice called out, 'What are you doing with our dinners, you monkeys – you?' And there was a big workman coming towards them, looking so cross and angry that those two bad children screamed and screamed, and because the workman was so roary they turned and ran and ran back down the road, and the workman ran after them as cross as cross. Weren't they frightened?

When they got back to where the other workmen were digging, those children were more frightened

than ever, because the big workman shouted to all the other workmen about what those naughty children had done with their dinners.

Yes, those poor workmen had put all their dinners under the hedge in the old mackintosh to keep them dry and safe until dinner-time. As well as being frightened, Bad Harry and my naughty little sister were very ashamed.

They were so ashamed that they did a most silly thing. When they heard the big workman telling the others about their dinners, those silly children ran and hid themselves in one of the pipes that the workmen were putting in the road.

My naughty little sister went first, and old Bad Harry went after her. Because my naughty little sister was so frightened she wriggled in and in the pipe, and Bad Harry came wriggling in after her, because he was frightened too.

And then a dreadful thing happened to my naughty little sister. That Bad Harry *stuck in the pipe* and he couldn't get any farther. He was quite a round fat boy, you see, and he stuck fast as fast in the pipe.

Then didn't those sillies howl and howl.

My little sister howled because she didn't want to go on and on down the roadmen's pipe on her own, and Bad Harry howled because he couldn't move at all.

It was all terrible, of course, but the roary workman rescued them very quickly. He couldn't reach Bad Harry with his arm, but he got a long hooky iron thing, and he hooked it in Bad Harry's belt, and he pulled and pulled, and presently he pulled Bad Harry out of the pipe. Wasn't it a good thing they had the hooky iron? And wasn't it a *very* good thing that

Bad Harry had a strong belt on his coat?

When Bad Harry was out, my little sister wriggled back and back, and came out too, and when she saw all the poor workmen who wouldn't have any dinner, she cried and cried, and told them what a sorry girl she was.

She told the workmen that she and Bad Harry hadn't known the mackintoshy bundle was their dinners, and Bad Harry said he was sorry too, and they were really so truly ashamed that the big workman said, 'Well, never mind this time. It's pay-day today, so we can send the boy for fish and chips instead,' and he told my little sister not to cry any more.

So my little sister stopped crying, and she and Bad Harry said they would never, never meddle and be inquisitive again.

The Elephant and the Bad Baby

ELFRIDA VIPONT

Once upon a time there was an Elephant.

And one day the Elephant went for a walk and he
met a Bad Baby. And the Elephant said to the Bad
Baby, 'Would you like a ride?' And the Bad Baby said,
'Yes.'

So the Elephant stretched out his trunk, and picked
up the Bad Baby and put him on his back, and they
went rumpeta, rumpeta, rumpeta, all down the road.

Very soon they met an ice-cream man.
And the Elephant said to the Bad Baby, 'Would you
like an ice-cream?' And the Bad Baby said, 'Yes.'

So the Elephant stretched out his trunk and took an ice-cream for himself and an ice-cream for the Bad Baby, and they went rumpeta, rumpeta, rumpeta, all down the road, with the ice-cream man running after.

Next they came to a pork butcher's shop.
And the Elephant said to the Bad Baby, 'Would you like a pie?' And the Bad Baby said, 'Yes.'
So the Elephant stretched out his trunk and took a pie for himself and a pie for the Bad Baby, and they went rumpeta, rumpeta, rumpeta, all down the road, with the ice-cream man and the pork butcher both running after.

Next they came to a baker's shop.
And the Elephant said to the Bad Baby, 'Would you like a bun?' And the Bad Baby said, 'Yes.'

So the Elephant stretched out his trunk and took a bun for himself and a bun for the Bad Baby, and they went rumpeta, rumpeta, rumpeta, all down the road, with the ice-cream man, and the pork butcher, and the baker all running after.

Next they came to a snack bar.

And the Elephant said to the Bad Baby, 'Would you like some crisps?' And the Bad Baby said, 'Yes.'

So the Elephant stretched out his trunk and took some crisps for himself and some crisps for the Bad Baby, and they went rumpeta, rumpeta, rumpeta, all down the road, with the ice-cream man, and the pork butcher, and the baker, and the snack bar man all running after.

Next they came to a grocer's shop.

And the Elephant said to the Bad Baby, 'Would you like a chocolate biscuit?' And the Bad Baby said, 'Yes.'

So the Elephant stretched out his trunk and took a chocolate biscuit for himself and a chocolate biscuit for the Bad Baby, and they went rumpeta, rumpeta, rumpeta, all down the road, with the ice-cream man, and the pork butcher, and the baker, and the snack bar man, and the grocer all running after.

Next they came to a sweet shop.
And the Elephant said to the Bad Baby, 'Would you like a lollipop?' And the Bad Baby said, 'Yes.'

So the Elephant stretched out his trunk and took a lollipop for himself and a lollipop for the Bad Baby, and they went rumpeta, rumpeta, rumpeta, all down the road, with the ice-cream man, and the pork butcher, and the baker, and the snack bar man, and the grocer, and the lady from the sweet shop all running after.

Next they came to a fruit barrow.
And the Elephant said to the Bad Baby, 'Would you like an apple?' And the Bad Baby said, 'Yes.'

19

So the Elephant stretched out his trunk and took an apple for himself and an apple for the Bad Baby, and they went rumpeta, rumpeta, rumpeta, all down the

road, with the ice-cream man, and the pork butcher, and the baker, and the snack bar man, and the grocer, and the lady from the sweet shop, and the barrow boy all running after.

Then the Elephant said to the Bad Baby, 'But you haven't once said please!' And then he said, 'You haven't ONCE said please!'
Then the Elephant sat down suddenly in the middle of the road and the Bad Baby fell off.

And the ice-cream man, and the pork butcher, and the baker, and the snack bar man, and the grocer, and the lady from the sweet shop, and the barrow boy all went BUMP into a heap.

And the Elephant said, 'But he never once said please!'

And the ice-cream man, and the pork butcher, and the baker, and the snack bar man, and the grocer, and the lady from the sweet shop, and the barrow boy all picked themselves up and said, 'Just fancy that! He never *once* said please!'

And the Bad Baby said: 'PLEASE! I want to go home to my Mummy!'

So the Elephant stretched out his trunk, and picked up the Bad Baby and put him on his back, and they went rumpeta, rumpeta, rumpeta, all down the road, with the ice-cream man, and the pork butcher, and the baker, and the snack bar man, and the grocer, and the lady from the sweet shop, and the barrow boy all running after.

21

When the Bad Baby's Mummy saw them, she said, 'Have you all come for tea?' And they all said, 'Yes, *please!*'

So they all went in and had tea, and the Bad Baby's Mummy made pancakes for everybody.

Then the Elephant went rumpeta, rumpeta, rumpeta, all down the road, with the ice-cream man, and the pork butcher, and the baker, and the snack bar man, and the grocer, and the lady from the sweet shop, and the barrow boy all running after.

And the Bad Baby went to bed.

'Fear-No-Bear'

DICK KING-SMITH

When Red Indian boys grow up to be Red Indian men, they are called 'braves', afraid of nothing.

But there was once a Red Indian boy who was afraid of nearly everything. So the tribe called him Yellow Liver.

One day Yellow Liver met a huge bear in the woods. He turned as white as a Red Indian can (which is sort of pink).

'Oh,' he whispered. 'What are you going to do?'

'Hug you to death,' said the bear.

'Why?'

'Because I'm in a very bad temper,' said the bear.

'Why?'

'Because I've got a sore head. Haven't you ever heard of a bear with a sore head? Come here and let me hug you to death.'

'But *why* have you got a sore head?' said Yellow Liver. The bear sat down and thought.

'Eating too many blueberries, I expect,' it said. 'They must have given me a headache.'

'But blueberries give you a tummy-ache, not a headache,' said Yellow Liver.

'Oh,' said the bear. 'Well, it can't be that. Maybe I got stung on the head when I was robbing a bees' nest.'

'But bee-stings don't hurt bears,' said Yellow Liver.

'Oh,' said the bear. 'Well, it can't be that. Perhaps I fell out of a tree and landed on my head.'

'But bears don't fall out of trees,' said Yellow Liver.

'You're right,' said the bear. 'They don't. Well, why do you think I've got a sore head?'

Yellow Liver took a deep breath.

'I don't think you have,' he said. 'I think you're imagining it.'

'Really?' said the bear. It shook its head a bit and looked thoughtful.

'D'you know,' it said, 'I do believe you're right. I don't think I have got a sore head after all.'

'So you aren't in a very bad temper?' said Yellow Liver.

'No.'

24

'So you don't want to hug me to death?'

'No,' said the bear. 'Not to death. But I'd like to give you a hug for curing my sore head.'

'It's very kind of you,' said Yellow Liver, 'but I'd rather you did me a favour.'

'Certainly,' said the bear. 'You name it.'

'Bend forward,' said Yellow Liver, and the bear bent forward so that the boy could whisper in its round furry ear.

The bear listened carefully.

'Really?' it said after a bit. 'You? Afraid? . . . I see, you want me to . . . yes . . . yes . . . what fun!'

What a panic there was when a huge bear walked into the camp that evening! And how amazed the tribe was when little Yellow Liver stepped forward to face it, Yellow Liver who was even afraid of mice! He punched the bear in the tummy, and then when it doubled up he punched it on the nose. When it turned away, he kicked its bottom. The bear gave a groan, clapped its paws to its behind, and ran off into the woods. It was grinning all over its face, but the tribe couldn't see that. They stood in silent wonder.

Then the chief came forward. He placed a single eagle's feather in Yellow Liver's headband. Then he turned to the tribe and said, 'No longer have we a boy called Yellow Liver. This is a brave, and his name is Fear-No-Bear.'

'His name is Fear-No-Bear,' chorused the tribe.

And the bear, watching through the trees, hugged itself for joy.

Two of Everything

ALICE RITCHIE

Mr and Mrs Hak-Tak were rather old and rather poor. They had a small house in a village among the mountains and a tiny patch of green land on the mountain side. Here they grew the vegetables which were all they had to live on, and when it was a good season and they did not need to eat up everything as soon as it was grown, Mr Hak-Tak took what they could spare in a basket to the next village which was a little larger than theirs and sold it for as much as he could get, and bought some oil for their lamp, and fresh seeds, and every now and then, but not often, a piece of cotton stuff to make new coats and trousers for himself and his wife. You can imagine they did not often get the chance to eat meat.

Now, one day it happened that when Mr Hak-Tak was digging in his precious patch, he unearthed a big brass pot. He thought it strange that it should have been there for so long without his having come across it before, and he was disappointed to find that it was empty; still, he thought they would find some use for it, so when he was ready to go back to the house in the evening he decided to take it with him. It was very big and heavy, and in his struggle to get his arms round it and raise it to a good position for carrying, his purse, which he always took with him in his belt, fell to the ground, and, to be quite sure he had it safe, he put it inside the pot and so staggered home with his load.

As soon as he got into the house Mrs Hak-Tak hurried from the inner room to meet him.

'My dear husband,' she said, 'whatever have you got there?'

'For a cooking-pot it is too big; for a bath a little too small,' said Mr Hak-Tak. 'I found it buried in our vegetable patch and so far it has been useful in carrying my purse home for me.'

'Alas,' said Mrs Hak-Tak, 'something smaller would have done as well to hold any money we have or are likely to have,' and she stooped over the pot and looked into its dark inside.

As she stooped, her hairpin – for poor Mrs Hak-Tak had only one hairpin for all her hair and it was made of carved bone – fell into the pot. She put in her hand to get it out again, and then she gave a loud cry which brought her husband running to her side.

'What is it?' he asked. 'Is there a viper in the pot?'

'Oh, my dear husband,' she cried, 'what can be the meaning of this? I put my hand into the pot to fetch out my hairpin and your purse, and look, I have brought out two hairpins and two purses, both exactly alike.'

'Open the purse. Open both purses,' said Mr Hak-Tak. 'One of them will certainly be empty.'

But not a bit of it. The new purse contained exactly the same number of coins as the old one – for that matter, no one could have said which was the new and which the old – and it meant, of course, that the Hak-Taks had exactly twice as much money in the evening as they had had in the morning.

'And two hairpins instead of one!' cried Mrs Hak-Tak, forgetting in her excitement to do up her hair, which was streaming over her shoulders. 'There is something quite unusual about this pot.'

'Let us put in the sack of lentils and see what happens,' said Mr Hak-Tak, also becoming excited.

They heaved in the bag of lentils and when they pulled it out again – it was so big it almost filled the pot – they saw another bag of exactly the same size waiting to be pulled out in its turn. So now they had two bags of lentils instead of one.

'Put in the blanket,' said Mr Hak-Tak. 'We need another blanket for the cold weather.' And, sure enough, when the blanket came out, there lay another behind it.

'Put my wadded coat in,' said Mr Hak-Tak, 'and then when the cold weather comes there will be one for you as well as for me. Let us put in everything we have in turn. What a pity we have no meat or tobacco, for it seems that the pot cannot make anything without a pattern.'

Then Mrs Hak-Tak, who was a woman of great intelligence, said, 'My dear husband, let us put the purse in again and again and again. If we take two purses out each time we put one in, we shall have enough money by tomorrow evening to buy everything we lack.'

'I am afraid we may lose it this time,' said Mr Hak-Tak, but in the end he agreed, and they dropped in the purse and pulled out two, then they added the new money to the old and dropped it in again and pulled out the larger amount twice over. After a while the floor was covered with old leather purses and they decided just to throw the money in by itself. It worked quite as well and saved trouble; every time, twice as much money came out as went in, and every time they added the new coins to the old and threw them all in together. It took some hours to tire of this game, but at last Mrs Hak-Tak said, 'My dear husband, there is no need for us to work so hard. We shall see to it that the pot does not run away, and we can always make more money as we want it. Let us tie up what we have.'

It made a huge bundle in the extra blanket and the Hak-Taks lay and looked at it for a long time before they slept, and talked of all the things they would buy and the improvements they would make in the cottage.

The next morning they rose early and Mr Hak-Tak filled a wallet with money from the bundle and set off for the big village to buy more things in one morning than he had bought in a whole fifty years.

Mrs Hak-Tak saw him off and then she tidied up the cottage and put the rice on to boil and had another look at the bundle of money, and made herself a whole set of new hairpins from the pot, and about twenty candles instead of the one which was all they had possessed up to now. After that she slept for a while, having been up so late the night before, but just before the time when her husband should be back, she awoke and went over to the pot. She dropped in a cabbage leaf to make sure it was still working properly, and when she took two leaves out she sat down on the floor and put her arms round it.

'I do not know how you came to us, my dear pot,' she said, 'but you are the best friend we ever had.'

Then she knelt up to look inside it, and at that moment her husband came to the door, and, turning quickly to see all the wonderful things he had bought, she overbalanced and fell into the pot.

Mr Hak-Tak put down his bundles and ran across and caught her by the ankles and pulled her out, but, Oh mercy, no sooner had he set her carefully on the floor than he saw the kicking legs of another Mrs Hak-Tak in the pot! What was he to do? Well, he could not leave her there, so he caught her ankles and pulled, and another Mrs Hak-Tak, so exactly like the first that no one could have told one from the other, stood beside them.

'Here's an extraordinary thing,' said Mr Hak-Tak, looking helplessly from one to the other.

'I will not have a second Mrs Hak-Tak in the house!' screamed the old Mrs Hak-Tak.

All was confusion. The old Mrs Hak-Tak shouted and wrung her hands and wept, Mr Hak-Tak was scarcely calmer, and the new Mrs Hak-Tak sat down on the floor as if she knew no more than they did what was to happen next.

'One wife is all *I* want,' said Mr Hak-Tak, 'but how could I have left her in the pot?'

'Put her back in it again!' cried Mrs Hak-Tak.

'What? And draw out two more?' said her husband.
'If two wives are too many for me, what should I do
with three? No! No!' He stepped back quickly as if he
was stepping away from the three wives and, missing
his footing, lo and behold, he fell into the pot!

Both Mrs Hak-Taks ran and each caught an ankle
and pulled him out and set him on the floor, and
there, Oh mercy, was another pair of kicking legs in
the pot! Again each caught hold of an ankle and
pulled, and soon another Mr Hak-Tak, so exactly like
the first that no one could have told one from the
other, stood beside them.

Now the old Mr Hak-Tak liked the idea of his
double no more than Mrs Hak-Tak had liked the idea
of hers. He stormed and raged and scolded his wife
for pulling him out of the pot, while the new Mr
Hak-Tak sat down on the floor beside the new Mrs
Hak-Tak and looked as if, like her, he did not know
what was going to happen next.

Then the old Mrs Hak-Tak had a very good idea.
'Listen, my dear husband,' she said, 'now, do stop
scolding and listen, for it is really a good thing that
there is a new one of you as well as a new one of me. It
means that you and I can go on in our usual way, and
these new people, who are ourselves and yet not
ourselves, can set up house together next door to us.'

And that is what they did. The old Hak-Taks built
themselves a fine new house with money from the
pot, and they built one just like it next door for the
new couple, and they lived together in the greatest
friendliness, because as Mrs Hak-Tak said, 'The new
Mrs Hak-Tak is really more than a sister to me, and

the new Mr Hak-Tak is really more than a brother to you.'

The neighbours were very much surprised, both at the sudden wealth of the Hak-Taks and at the new couple who resembled them so strongly that they must, they thought, be very close relations of whom they had never heard before. They said: 'It looks as if the Hak-Taks, when they so unexpectedly became rich, decided to have two of everything, even of themselves, in order to enjoy their money more.'

Monkeying About

retold by STEPHEN CORRIN

'Caps for sale! Caps for sale!' shouted the pedlar as he walked through the streets.

But where were the caps?

Not on a cart, not on a barrow, not on a sack on his back, not even on a tray strapped to his shoulders. This pedlar carried his caps, every single one of them, in an enormously high pile on the top of his own flat cap – on the top of his head.

First came the blue caps, on top of these the yellow caps, then the orange ones, then purple ones and then, on the very top of all, the bright red ones. The pedlar, of course, had to walk very straight and carefully so as not to spill the caps.

Usually the pedlar did quite a good trade, for people were amused by the way he walked and by the clever way he could pick out any colour a customer chose without even looking up or upsetting the pile. What happened was he used a special little stick with a flat top and, with this in his left hand, he held the whole pile balanced while his right hand skilfully whisked out the colour required. His right hand seemed able to stretch very high up indeed!

One day, however, for some odd reason, not a

single person came out to buy a cap. The pedlar walked up and down the streets, back and forth, back and forth, shouting, 'Caps for sale! Caps for sale!' at the top of his voice – but there were no customers.

At last the pedlar thought to himself, 'Well, one gets good days and one gets bad days. Anyway, this will be a good chance for me to take a rest and enjoy a snooze in the fresh country air.'

So off he set to a nearby wood. He sat himself down very carefully, leaning his back against the trunk of a stout oak tree, and within seconds, believe it or not, he was fast asleep in the warm sunshine, the caps still piled high on his head.

How long he slept he had no idea, but when he awoke he straightaway put up his hand to feel for his caps. Strange to relate, only his own flat cap was there. What a shock!

He looked to his left. No caps.

He looked to his right. No caps.

He looked behind. No caps.

And, of course, he looked in front. No caps.

So he stood up and walked round and round the tree but – still no caps.

Then he looked up into the branches of the tree above him and – just try to guess what he saw: monkeys, monkeys, monkeys and monkeys, chattering their heads off and laughing with great glee. AND EVERY MONKEY HAD A CAP ON HIS HEAD.

Some had a red cap on,

some a yellow one,

some an orange one,

some a blue one

and some a purple one.

'Hey, you monkeys! Give me back my caps!' shouted the pedlar, shaking his fist at them. But the monkeys only shook their fists back at him, chuckling, 'Tseek, tseek, tseek' and 'Hee, hee, hee!'

'You cheeky rascals!' he shouted again. 'Give me my caps back at once!' But the monkeys only continued their 'tseek, tseek, tseek' and 'hee, hee, hee'. They seemed to be enjoying the fun hugely. The pedlar shouted himself hoarse and shook both his fists at them, but the monkeys only shook *their* fists back at him and tseek, tseek tseeked and hee, hee hee'd for all their worth.

By now the pedlar was almost beside himself with rage. He stamped his foot and screamed, 'You give me back my caps or else . . .!'

But the monkeys only stamped *their* feet back at him.

At his wits' end the pedlar took off his own flat cap and flung it to the ground, helpless with anger and impatience. And just as he was about to walk away, the monkeys DID EXACTLY AS HE HAD DONE. Each one pulled off the cap he was wearing and threw it to the ground. Down came all the caps – yellow, orange, blue, purple and red – scattered all over the place. What copy-cats! Or should we say, what copy-monkeys!

The pedlar picked them all up, one by one, and placed them on top of his own flat cap as before – the blue, the yellow, the orange, the purple and the bright red. He then walked back into the town, up and down the streets, merrily shouting, 'Caps for sale! Caps for sale!' And this time he was lucky.

He sold the lot.

The Giraffe who Saw to the End of the World

BRIAN PATTEN

In a jungle that was almost a forest, and in a forest that was almost a wood, and in a wood that was almost a garden, there once lived an elephant and a flower and a pig and a giraffe and a kuputte-bird. There was also a hyena there and a plinkinplonk and monkeys as well; and of course there was a forest of moonbeams, and a silver ant that dreamt of silence, and a river that told the strangest stories.

Sometimes the giraffe came to the hill where the elephant and the flower lived. The giraffe had a very long neck, and when it stood on top of the hill and stretched its neck it could see over the trees and mountains to the end of the world.

One day the flower asked, 'What is the end of the world like?'

'Beautiful,' said the giraffe.

'What lives there?' asked the elephant.

'Giraffes, of course,' answered the giraffe.

The elephant had always thought elephants lived at the end of the world. And the flower had always thought only flowers could live in such a faraway place.

'Isn't there even one elephant there?' asked the elephant.

The giraffe stretched its neck as hard as it could. It looked across the trees and the mountains for a long time, and then said, 'No, only giraffes.'

'Maybe the giraffes are hiding a few flowers,' suggested the flower.

'Most certainly not,' said the giraffe.

'He's not telling the truth,' said a voice above them. It was the sparrow, who had been sitting all the time on the giraffe's head. 'I can see the end of the world a little better than he can, and it's full of sparrows. Very large sparrows, even larger than eagles.'

41

The giraffe said it had forgotten to mention sparrows, as they were smaller than giraffes.

'But there are definitely no elephants or flowers there,' it insisted.

'You're quite right,' agreed the sparrow.

The elephant and the flower decided to go for a walk instead of listening to the other two creatures, who were now boasting loudly. On their walk they asked all the creatures they met, 'What do you think lives at the end of the world?' And the ant-eater said ant-eaters, and the snake said snakes, and the pig said pigs, and the lizard said lizards. And every single creature thought the only things that lived at the end of the world were just like themselves, only a little larger.

Later in the afternoon when the elephant and the flower returned to the hill, they found all the creatures they had met on their walk gathered round the giraffe. The giraffe and the sparrow had agreed that only giraffes and sparrows lived at the end of the world. They were telling the other creatures that there were lakes and forests and rivers and trees and even weeds there. But no other animals.

The animals were very indignant. 'We want to see for ourselves,' they shouted.

'You can't,' said the giraffe. 'You're not tall enough.'

'You can't,' said the sparrow. 'You've got no wings.'

Then the pig had one of its rare ideas. 'We'll all climb up the giraffe's neck and see for ourselves,' it said.

The giraffe didn't like the idea, especially as it was the pig's.

'It's a stupid idea,' it said. 'Fancy a pig trying to make a suggestion of any kind. It's bound to fail.'

But the other animals did not agree. They wanted to see the end of the world for themselves and they shouted and grunted so much that the giraffe had to agree to the pig's idea.

So first the snake climbed up. 'Just as I thought,' it said. 'The end of the world is full of snakes.'

'Nonsense,' squeaked the pig, and he began to climb up the giraffe, slipping every now and then. He clung to the giraffe's ears and shouted down: 'The snake's lying as usual. The end of the world's full of pigs. Very beautiful pigs. I can even see a King Pig sitting on a throne.'

'Rubbish,' shouted the ant-eater. 'Let's have a look.'

And when the ant-eater had reached the top it said, 'Why, what glorious ant-eaters there are! And so many ants to eat as well.'

'I still think that they're all wrong,' said the sparrow, who was fluttering above the ant-eater. 'I'm the furthest up, and so have the clearest view. It's definitely sparrows.'

And so the creatures began to argue.

'High up is far enough to see the end of the world,' they shouted at the sparrow. And the pig was so angry it nearly fell down.

'Take your feet out of my ears,' it squeaked at the ant-eater, who was sitting unsteadily on top of it. 'And take your hoof off my head,' shouted the snake.

As they argued, other creatures began to climb up the giraffe's neck. For miles and miles around, the jungle was full of talk and speculation about what lived at the end of the world.

Soon there was a gigantic pile of creatures on top of the giraffe's head. There were snakes and ant-eaters and pigs and frogs and monkeys and the white rabbit as well. Only the larger jungle creatures stayed on the ground with the elephant and the flower. They thought it a rather undignified heap, and knew quite well what lived at the end of the world.

The giraffe's neck was beginning to ache and strain.

All the time the creatures had been clambering over each other, a caterpillar had been slowly working its way up the giraffe's neck. It climbed on to the pig's head and stood upright. It was a very timid caterpillar and was a bit afraid of saying that the world was full of caterpillars. But it didn't have to anyway. The weight of all the creatures had become too much for the giraffe. It staggered on its feet, then tumbled down the hill. The creatures fell down on top of it in a huge heap. They all wriggled and groaned. And when they had untangled themselves they surrounded the caterpillar.

'It's your fault,' said the pig. 'It was your weight that made us fall. Now you'll have to settle the argument.'

The caterpillar was very afraid of the animals, and it didn't want to make them any angrier by saying the end of the world was full of caterpillars.

So it said: 'The end of the world's full of everything.'

Though the other creatures did not believe it, they were so relieved that it wasn't full of caterpillars they agreed that maybe the caterpillar could see best after all. And so they went home happy, leaving the flower and the elephant alone on the hill. It was getting dark anyway.

The Clever Little Girl and the Bear

Russian Folk Tale
retold by STEPHEN CORRIN

Natasha lived with her mother and father in a little wooden house right at the edge of the forest. One fine morning Natasha and some of her friends went into the forest to pick berries and Natasha, wandering off just a little, was happy to find a thick bush simply loaded with luscious ripe berries. She got so busy and excited plucking the mouth-watering fruits that she quite forgot the time. So when she had filled her basket to overflowing and she looked around for her friends, they were nowhere to be seen. She wandered about looking for them, here, there and everywhere, and in the end she found she was lost and had no idea which path led back to her home.

Through a clearing in the trees she espied a little cottage in the distance, and decided to go there and ask for help to find her way back. She knocked and knocked and knocked, but there was no reply, so she pushed the door open. Seeing a cosy-looking stove, she sat down next to it to have a rest and get warm, for the evening air was now quite cool.

After a little while, in walked a big brown bear. It was *his* cottage and this was where he lived. He was quite delighted to find the little girl there and asked her her name.

46

'I'm called Natasha,' she said, but inside she felt rather scared, for he was a BIG bear and his voice, though friendly, was gruff.

'What a pretty name,' said the bear. 'A little girl like you is just what I need to keep my house nice and tidy and cook my meals. So please stay here, my dear, and *please* don't try to run away while I'm out, for if you do I shall have to run after you and catch you and perhaps eat you up.'

Natasha was terribly frightened and began to cry. 'Whatever am I to do?' she thought. 'Perhaps for the time being I'd better do what the bear asks and work out a plan to make my escape.'

So for a few days she looked after the bear's home, kept it nice and tidy, and cooked his meals while he was away in the forest. But all the time, day and night, she kept thinking of different ways of getting back to her father and mother. And one morning she hit upon a clever idea.

'Bear,' she said to him one evening after he had enjoyed the meal she had prepared for him, 'could I please ask you to take a present from me to my dear parents?'

'Gladly,' replied the big brown bear.

So Natasha baked a very large batch of tarts and put them in an extra-large-size basket which she found in a corner of the kitchen.

'Of course you'll be able to carry this basket of tarts on your back,' she told the big brown bear. 'But please promise me that you'll not eat a single one on the way. I'll climb up on to the roof to keep an eye on you.'

'Of course, I promise,' said the big brown bear.

While he was getting ready to leave, Natasha crept quietly into the basket, making herself as tiny as possible so as to be quite hidden by the large batch of tarts.

Then the big brown bear hoisted the basket on to his broad back and set off for the village where Natasha's parents lived.

'Nice lot of tarts that girl must have baked,' he thought, staggering just a tiny bit under the weight. He sat down on a tree-stump to rest for a while, his mouth watering as he thought of the delicious tarts so near to hand. He hummed a little tune and found himself singing:

> Now in safety, out of view,
> I see no harm to steal a few.

And this he promptly did. But from under the tarts came Natasha's voice:

> You may think you're out of view,
> But I've just seen you steal a few.
> Your roof, brown bear, is good and high,
> So nothing 'scapes my eagle eye.

The big brown bear got up rather sharply, somewhat taken aback.

'My my,' he growled to himself, 'she can certainly see a long way.' But after walking a little way he sat down again, thinking that this time he couldn't possibly be seen, and took another tart out of the basket. But after he'd taken only one bite, out came that voice again:

>Caught you again, you greedy bear!
>Stealing presents isn't fair.
>Not another! Don't you dare!

The bear gave a jump and exclaimed:

>That girl, she must have magic sight.
>She's really put me in a fright.
>She seems to see right through the trees.
>She's left me trembling at the knees!

He now set off in great haste to the village, and when he got to Natasha's house, he set down the basket and knocked at the door. Four dogs appeared, barking their heads off. They had smelled the bear AND Natasha too. They rushed at him and snapped threateningly at his legs. The big brown bear was so scared that he took to his heels and escaped into the forest as fast as he could.

When Natasha's mother and father opened the door, out jumped the little girl and fell happily into their joyful arms.

What a clever little girl she was!

The Little Red Engine Gets a Name

DIANA ROSS

Once upon a time there was a Little Red Engine. It lived in a shed with a Big Black Engine and a Big Green Engine at the junction of Taddlecombe, where the great main line to the North and the great main line to the South met the little branch line on which the Little Red Engine was running.

The Big Black Engine was called *Pride o' the North*, written in letters of gold on its side, and the Big Green Engine was called *Beauty of the South*; but the Little Red Engine had no name at all, only a number written in black, 394, for it only worked on a branch line, and the others were Main Line engines.

How sad was the Little Red Engine! Every night when it got home from its run it heard the other engines boasting of what they had seen.

'Ah!' they would say. 'You don't know what you are missing. All you ever see are empty fields and cows and a village here and there, and your only excitements are your ten level crossings, and everyone knows that they are out of date.

'You should just see what we see every day of our lives! Towns, towns. Can you even imagine a town? Some are big and some are small, but a hundred of

51

your villages would hardly fill one street! And some have castles and some fine churches, and some are full of factories and dockyards and warehouses. And as for the stations! Why, the least have a dozen platforms.'

And the Little Red Engine could only sigh with envy, because how could it tell when the others were exaggerating?

'And as for the tunnels,' they would say, 'Whooooo, there *is* a thrill. You take a deep breath, WHEEEOOOOO, Wurra Burra, Wurra Burra, Wurra Burra, Whoooeeeooo; and there you are out

on the other side. And as for the bridges, Clack-a-tack, Clack-a-tack, Clack-a-tack till you're over. Give us the main line,' they said, and sighed contentedly before they went to sleep.

And the Little Red Engine would stay awake and think to himself:

'How lucky they are! I wish I could see the things that they have seen, I wish I could go through a tunnel, I wish I could run on a bridge. I like my branch line very much, and I shouldn't like to leave it. But if only once I could be a Main Line engine. Only once and then I should be content.'

And it would let off steam in such a sigh, Whooooeeeee, and would go to sleep and would dream of the Great Main Line.

Now one day in the winter there was an awful storm. The wind blew, the snow fell, and a tree was blown down and fell across the great main line to the South. And the Big Green Engine, *Beauty of the South*, went rushing right into it, dada-da-da, dada-da-da, dada-da-da BOOM! And jumped the line and over it fell, and the wheels went whrrrrrr, and the steam went whooooshhhhh, and though nobody was hurt, there the engine lay by the side of the track.

'It will take three days to move her,' said the driver, scratching his head, and sat down on the lines to wait for help to come.

At the same time the Big Black Engine, *Pride o' the North*, went puffing through the storm, chuffa chuffa chuffff, chuffa chuffa chuffff, and the snow fell fast and it could not see and it did not know that a snowdrift had blocked the great main line to the North and into the snowdrift it ran HOOOSH!

And there it was stuck fast. And the snow fell and covered it up. And the men who came to dig it out shook their heads and blew on their fingers.

'We'll never get her out under three days at least.'

And they sat down and drank cocoa to keep themselves warm.

But what a misfortune!

For the King himself was staying near Taddlecombe Junction. And he had to get home by the very next day.

'Matters of state. Matters of state, Very Important.'

And here were the main line engines useless for three days more.

So the King sent messengers to the Station Master.

'Come, sir, come. Surely you can think of something. Have you no other engine fit to do the work?'

And the Station Master shook his head, but as he did so he heard a little whistle from the engine shed.

'Wait a minute,' he said. And ran to look inside.

There he saw the Little Red Engine, its face shining.

'Chuffa chuff chuff. Chuffa chuff chuff. Let me go. I can do it. Let me go. I really can.'

'Well, the Great Main Line is a difficult business. Are you sure you could manage? You've never had main line experience.' And the Station Master stood in doubt.

'Chuffa chuff chuff. I'm sure I can.'

And the Little Red Engine looked so eager.

'We can but try,' said the Station Master. And he ran and told the King's messengers he thought he could manage something.

So they fixed a special coach to the Little Red

Engine, newly painted with the King's arms upon it, and the King would ride in this. And behind this coach were seven first-class carriages and all the King's friends were going to ride in these. And behind that again were ten big luggage vans, and all the King's luggage would hardly go in these.

And that was a bigger load than the Little Red Engine had ever pulled before.

'Are you sure you can do it?' asked the Station Master anxiously.

'Chuffa chuff chuff,' cried the Little Red Engine. And its driver leant out of the cab.

'Don't you worry. The Little Red Engine can do it.'

Then the King came along.

When he saw the Little Red Engine –

'Is this the best you can do?' he asked.

'I'm afraid it is, Your Majesty.'

'Well, let's hope there will be no accidents.'

And in he got, with all his friends, and the whistle blew and away they went.

'I'm a main line train and I'm carrying the King. WHOOOEEEOOO.' And out it ran on the Great Main Line.

The storm of the day before was over now, and the sun shone, and the sky was blue, and the Little Red Engine went puffing along the line.

'I'm a main line train and I'm carrying the King. WHOOOEEEOOO.'

And then they came to a tunnel, the first it had ever been through. It took a deep breath:

'WHOOOEEEOOO.

'Burra wurra, burra wurra, burra wurra. WHOOOEEEOOO.'

And there they were out on the other side.

'I've been through a tunnel. I'm a main line train and I'm carrying the King. WHOOOEEEOOO,' sang the Little Red Engine.

They came to a river, very wide and very deep. Over the river went a bridge. The very first bridge the Little Red Engine had come to.

Clack-a-tack-tack. Clack-a-tack-tack. Clack-a-tack-tack. And there they were on the other side of the river.

'I've been through a tunnel and over a bridge. I'm a main line train and I'm carrying the King. WHOOOEEEOOO,' sang the Little Red Engine.

It came to a town, the first it had seen. In the middle was a castle and soldiers were drilling. Their band was playing and the gun went off Boom Boom!

'I've been through a tunnel and over a bridge. I've been through a town with a castle in the middle. I'm a main line train and I'm carrying the King, WHOOOEEEOOO.'

They came to a town with a church in the middle. The bells were ringing, 'Oh! All good people come to church. Oh! All good people come to church.'

'I've been through a tunnel and over a bridge. I've been through a town with a castle in the middle. I've been through a town with a church in the middle. I'm a main line train and I'm carrying the King. WHOOOEEEOOO.'

They came to a town with factories in the middle, and canals with barges and cranes and wharves and lorries.

'HEEEEEOOOOOOO,' screamed the factory whistle. Clang clang clang clang, went the noise of the

57

machines. Hoot, toot, went the tugs on the canal.

'I've been through a tunnel and over a bridge. I've been through a town with a castle in the middle. I've been through a town with a church in the middle. I've been through a town with factories in the middle. I'm a main line train and I'm carrying the King. WHOOOEEEOOO.'

And soon they came near London town. On every side were railway lines, and electric trains which hadn't even an engine were running past and looking at the Little Red Engine curiously.

'What a funny little engine to be out on the main line, and pulling the King too, and it hasn't even a name!' And the suburban electric trains sniffed as they went past, but they really had no right to for they had no names either.

And all along the line were the backs of houses. Houses and houses and houses and houses. The Little Red Engine hadn't thought there could be so many in the world.

Then in they came to an *enormous* station. A dozen platforms? There were over twenty! And all the people, and porters and trucks and taxis! 'Make way please, make way. Mind your backs. Ting Ting.' And boys who shouted 'Paper! Paper! Chocolates, papers, cigarettes!'

And as they drew into the platform, 'WHOOOEEEOOO. I've been through a tunnel and over a bridge. I've been through a town with a castle in the middle. I've been through a town with a church in the middle. I've been through a town with factories in the middle. I'm a main line train and I'm carrying the King. And here I am in London town. Chufffff-fff.' And the Little Red Engine pulled up at the platform.

When the King got out of his coach all the people came crowding around him. 'Just a moment, please.' And he waved them aside.

Then he walked up the platform to the Little Red Engine.

'I never thought you would do it,' he said. 'A very fine performance. You are not a moment late.'

Then, turning to the Station Master of the big London terminus, 'This Little Red Engine is now a Main Line Engine. You must give it a name and paint it on its sides in gold. Call it *Royal Red*. And add *By Special Appointment*.'

And they did as he said.

So when the Little Red Engine went home, how happy and proud it was. For on its side in letters of gold was written *Royal Red, by Special Appointment to His Majesty The King*.

And when the two other big engines came back

what was their surprise.

For when they began to boast again, the Little Red Engine said:

'I've been through a tunnel and over a bridge. I've been through a town with a castle in the middle. I've been through a town with a church in the middle. I've been through a town with factories in the middle. I've even been to London town. I'm a MAIN LINE ENGINE and I've carried the King. My name is *Royal Red. By Special Appointment.* And now I'm quite happy on my own branch line. WHOOOEEEEEOOO.'

And the *Royal Red* went happily to sleep.

The Little Girl who Got Out of Bed the Wrong Side

RUTH AINSWORTH

There was once a little girl who got out of bed on the wrong side. Oh, how cross she was! Cross as two sticks! She made a terrible fuss getting dressed. She put her tights on back to front and she complained that her jersey was tickly. She put her feet into the wrong shoes.

When she came down to breakfast, things were even worse. Her porridge was too hot. The milk was too cold. And her banana had black specks in it.

'I shan't eat my horrid breakfast,' said the little girl.

The kitten hid under the sofa and the puppy went into the brush cupboard and closed his eyes and pretended he wasn't there. The little girl was rather sorry, because she liked playing with the kitten and the puppy.

Everyone in the house left her alone and hoped she would soon feel better.

During the morning, her mother was busy making the Christmas puddings. When she had the mixture ready in her big mixing bowl, it looked delicious and smelt even more delicious. She asked the little girl if she would like to give the puddings a stir and have a wish.

'You'd better wish to be a happy girl,' said her mother.

The little girl took the tall wooden spoon and stirred round and round, and as she stirred she *did* wish to be a happy girl. The wish came true even before she had licked the spoon. The kitten came out from under the sofa, and the puppy came out of the brush cupboard, and they had a lovely game all over the house.

When lunch-time came, the little girl ate all her first course, which was fish fingers, and all her pudding, which was apple crumble. Afterwards, she went upstairs for her nap and the kitten and the puppy had their naps, too. When she woke up, she was very careful to get out of her bed on the *right* side.

My Puppy

AILEEN FISHER

It's funny
my puppy
knows just how I feel.

When I'm happy
he's yappy
and squirms like an eel.

When I'm grumpy
he's slumpy
and stays at my heel.

It's funny
my puppy
knows such a great deal.

Brown Bear in a Brown Chair

IRINA HALE

There once was a Brown Bear who lived in a brown chair. He was sat upon very often, because you couldn't see he was there.

'I'm feeling so flat,' he said, 'when really a bear should feel happy and fat.'

One day, he had a good idea, so he called Maggie, the little girl whose Bear he was.

'I must have a ribbon round my neck,' he said, 'so that people can see I'm here.'

Maggie got him a yellow ribbon off a chocolate box.

Bear sat happily on his chair. A mother bird on the window-sill saw him. She cheeped to her children, 'Look! There's a bear in that room with no clothes on! Only a yellow ribbon round his neck, and nothing else!'

Bear began to feel he was wearing too little.

'I hope those nasty birds don't find any worms for breakfast today,' he said.

'I have to have some trousers now,' Bear told Maggie.

So she cut the legs off an old pair of stripey pants to Bear's size and hemmed them. But they were too tight and made his tummy stick out.

'Aren't I well-dressed?' Bear said.

Just then, the cat went by and said, 'How can you be well-dressed if you don't have shoes on? Bears like you don't deserve to sit on comfy armchairs!'

(The cat really wanted the chair all to himself.)

Bear stamped his feet till Maggie came. 'I've got to have a pair of shoes now, or I'll never be really well-dressed.'

So Maggie had to take the shoes off her doll for Bear. The doll was very cross and gave a big sneeze.

'I shall get a bad cold now, all because of you!' she said to Bear. But he pretended not to hear.

Suddenly Bear saw a little mouse, peeping at him over the chair.

It squeaked, 'Oh what a fat, lazy bear! Just lying around on a chair all day! Not like us poor mice. We have to work hard just to find one tiny crumb!'

So Bear said to Maggie, 'Now I must have a shirt, to cover my tummy that's sticking out!'

Maggie sat down and made him a shirt, sewing with large stitches. It took a bit of time, but at last, there it was, finished. Bear felt very proud.

'Am I dressed right, now?' Bear said to the poodle, who was watching him. He stood on his head, feet up, to show off his new shoes.

The poodle sniffed. 'You can't be in fashion without a hat! Didn't you know? All smart people have hats!'

So Bear wanted a hat next. But what excuse could he find this time?

'Maggie!' he said. 'I feel cold on my head . . .'

Maggie looked at him and went off to find a little sun-hat in the bottom of a drawer. She had worn it when she was a baby. It was just Bear's size.

'There, is that all now?' she asked, putting his hat on. 'You are really becoming quite a Bothersome Bear!'

Bear sat with his hat on, thinking hard. What else was there that he must have and didn't have?

Just then the parrot woke up on his perch. He fixed a wicked eye on Bear. Suddenly he screeched, 'You do look silly! Just like a clown dressed up for the circus!'

Bear was very upset. Though he was all dressed up, he only made people laugh!

Then he had his second good idea – to throw off all those horrid clothes quickly! They were making him feel very uncomfortable and not at all like himself.

Up went his hat into the air. Off with those tight trousers! Shoes – away with them – one, two! He felt better and better every minute! The shirt and the ribbon went last. All the animals cheered.

Maggie's mother made a new cover for the old brown chair. Bear said, 'A brown bear shows up well on a flowery chair. I won't be sat on by mistake any more!'

But there was a bit of left-over flowery material. Maggie's mother made Bear a little dress out of it. So there he was again, a bear wearing the same pattern as the chair. And everyone was sure to sit on him as before.

Bear didn't have time to be worried for long. At bedtime Maggie told him: 'Don't be sad, Bear. I promise you won't get sat on any more – I'll always remember you are there.'

The Leopard that Lost a Spot

ANITA HEWETT

Leopard lay beneath a tree, carefully counting his
spots. There were ninety-eight, sooty black on his soft
yellow fur.

'Oh do stop counting your silly spots,' Monkey
called from the branches above.

'Eighty-five, eighty-six, eighty-seven, eighty-eight,'
counted Leopard.

'Silly Leopard!' Monkey said. 'I'm tired of hearing
you counting all day.' And away he ran across the
forest to the house where Man lived.

Man was painting a yellow fence, and Monkey
watched from behind a thorn bush. When noon came
and the sun grew hot, Man put down his pot of paint
and went inside his house to rest. This was what
Monkey had waited for! He snatched up the yellow
paint and the brush, and scampered back across the
forest to the tree where Leopard still counted his
spots. He hid the paint in the long grass, climbed the
tree, sat on a branch, and waited.

Leopard counted his spots once more. Then he
said: 'They are all there. That is good. I will sleep.'

As soon as Leopard began to snore, Monkey came
quietly down the tree. He picked up the pot of yellow

paint and tiptoed close to the leopard. He looked at
Leopard's black spots very carefully, until he found
the biggest of all. He dipped the brush in the yellow
paint, and painted over that big black spot so that it
did not show. Then he hid the paint in the grass,
climbed up into the tree, sat on a branch, and waited.

When Leopard awoke, he yawned three times.
Then he started counting his spots.

'One, two, three,' he said, and counted up to
ninety-seven.

'Only ninety-seven! Just ninety-seven!' he cried. 'I
ought to have ninety-eight. I've lost a spot! Oh what
shall I do? I've lost a spot!'

Monkey, on his branch above, laughed so much
that he nearly choked.

'Where is my ninety-eighth spot?' cried Leopard.
'Where is it? Where is my spot?'

Then he looked wise.

'I expect I am sitting on it,' he said, and he stood up
and snuffled about in the grass.

71

Monkey, on his branch above, laughed so much that his sides ached. Leopard ran off through the forest, calling: 'Where is my spot? I must find my spot.'

Porcupine looked for it, Elephant looked for it, Lion looked for it, Snake looked for it. They searched high and they searched low, but they could not find that missing spot. Then thunder rolled across the sky and drops of rain splashed on Leopard. Porcupine, Elephant, Lion, and Snake took shelter, but Leopard

stayed out in the pouring rain because he was anxious to find his spot. When the storm passed and the sun shone, Leopard was tired and exceedingly wet.

'I will rest for a while beneath my tree, and the sun will dry my fur,' he said. Then a dreadful fear came into his mind. Perhaps he had lost another spot!

'One, two, three,' he said, and counted up to ninety-eight.

'Ninety-eight!' he cried in delight. 'It's come back again! My spot has come back! Now how could a spot get lost like that, and then find its own way back?'

Monkey, on his branch above, laughed so much that he nearly fell out of the tree. But he did not tell Leopard about the paint, or that the rain had washed it off so that the spot could show again.

'Strange!' said Leopard. 'Exceedingly strange!'

Then Monkey laughed and laughed so much that he really did fall out of the tree. He did not fall on the soft leaves. Nor did he fall in the long grass. He fell where he deserved to fall – in the pot of yellow paint!

74

The Girl and the Crocodile

LEILA BERG

This is a story about a promise. And this is the way *I* tell it.

Once upon a time there was a girl who was sitting on a big stone by the river, and watching the fish. And while she was watching, she felt someone was watching *her*. You know how you do?

She looked up, and there was a crocodile. Staring. The little girl wasn't the least bit bothered. She just stared back.

'I bet you can't catch fish,' said the girl.

'Oh, easy-peasy!' said the crocodile. 'Of course I can.'

'Catch me some,' said the little girl.

'All right,' said the crocodile. 'But you'll have to give me something if I do.'

Well, the girl thought.

'I don't mind,' she said. 'On Saturday my Dad's having a birthday party, and if you come in the morning before it starts I'll give you a bottle of beer.'

'Oh, terrific!' said the crocodile. 'That's what I really do like!'

He caught a fish for the girl, and one for her Mum and one for her Dad, and she thanked him most politely like her mother had always taught her, and said, 'Don't forget now, will you? Saturday's the day,' – never thinking for a moment he'd remember. And off she went.

And the crocodile stayed in the river, crossing off his calendar every morning, and saying, 'Today's Monday.' 'Today's Tuesday.' 'Today's Wednesday.' 'Today's Thursday.' 'Today's Friday.' 'Today's Saturday. *Birthday Party*!'

And out he came, ever so excited, and swished his tail up the High Street, past the café, past the sweet shop, past the place where they sell cars in matchboxes, and into the little girl's street, and he knocked at the door with his tail. Frump! Frump!

The girl came to the door, because there was no one else in the house. Her Mum and Dad were out getting things for the party.

'Oh!' she said. 'Oh! I never thought . . .!'

Well, you don't, do you?

'I've come for my present,' said the crocodile.

'Oh, come in, come in,' she said, all in a fluster. 'Don't stand there on the step. I'll get into terrible trouble.'

So he came in, trying quite truly not to knock everything down with his strong tail, which was difficult because the kitchen was small.

And the girl kept saying, 'Be quiet! Oh, mind that cup!'

Then the girl got a bottle of beer from a box under the sink, and he emptied it down his throat with a plopping sound. Perlopp. Perlopp. Perlopp.

And when the last drop had gone down, he began to sing a little song.

Crocodiles are not really bad,
Sometimes they're happy and sometimes they're sad.
Whoops!

'Oh, do be quiet!' said the girl. 'I shall get into terrible trouble if my Mum and Dad hear you.'

'But I like singing,' said the crocodile. 'People always sing at parties. Give me some more beer.'

'There isn't any more,' she said.

'Oh, you story!' he said. 'There are hundreds of bottles under the sink. I *saw* them.'

So she gave him another bottle to keep him quiet, and he gurgled that one down too. Perlopp. Perlopp.

And he sang again:

Crocodiles are not really bad,
Sometimes they're happy, and sometimes they're sad.
Whoops!

'Oh, for heaven's sake be *quiet*!' she said. 'We'll have everyone here in a minute, and won't they be mad at me!'

'Well, give me another bottle,' he said. So she gave him another.

And he gurgled that one down too, and sang again, beating time with his tail on the dinner-gong that the little girl's Dad had picked up at an auction last Wednesday.

Crocodiles are not really bad,
Sometimes they're happy and sometimes they're sad.
Whoops!

And then he wandered out of the house, dancing on

his hind legs, and clapping with his front feet, and bumping into the chrysanthemums that the girl's Dad had planted last Sunday.

And the little girl ran after him, crying, 'Oh, do be quiet! You'll get me into terrible trouble!'

And just as he went past the pond, the girl managed to push him in. But he got out, and she pushed him in again, and he got out again, and began to chase her right down the street, and past the place where you get the little cars in matchboxes, and past the sweet shop, *and* past the café. And he was singing:

Crocodiles are not really bad,
Sometimes they're happy and sometimes they're sad.
Whoops!

79

and she was shouting (well, you would, wouldn't you?) right down to the bottom of the hill.

Now all the Mums and Dads were coming out of their gates to go to her Dad's birthday party, because it was nearly time, you see.

And her Auntie was there. And her Auntie was very sensible and brave and quick-thinking, and she spread out her arms wide and stood right in his path, to stop him chasing the girl (whose name, by the way, was Amanda).

But it was no use. The crocodile just floppered her down with his tail, giving her a headache for weeks, and went on chasing.

But Amanda's Mum and Dad, who were just coming out of the cake shop, and all the other Mums and Dads coming out of their gates, heard the *extraordinary* noise, and came rushing up, and they stood one behind the other, and they caught the crocodile in all their hands, and they held him up in the air high above their heads, and they ran down with him to the river, and they threw him in. Flup splash!

Then they all came back to the girl, puffing a little, and her Mum and Dad said, 'Whatever were you doing with that crocodile? Now tell the truth!'

And the girl said, 'Well, you know those fishes we ate on Sunday. Well, that crocodile caught them for me, and I promised I'd give him some beer as a present.'

'*You promised him some beer*!' said all the Mums and Dads.

(And her Auntie said, 'Oh my poor head!')

And her Mum and Dad said, 'Amanda! Don't you know that we never ask crocodiles to parties!'

And all night long, when the party was finished, and all the people gone home, and the last gate shut again, they could hear the old crocodile still singing away to himself in the river, beating time with his tail on the big stone and clapping his front feet.

> *Crocodiles are not really bad,*
> *Sometimes they're happy and sometimes they're sad.*
> *Whoops!*

Snip snap snover,
That story's over.

The Magic Umbrella

ROSE FYLEMAN

There was once a wizard who had a magic umbrella.
One night he went to a meeting of wizards and
witches in the market place, and when it was over he
forgot his umbrella and left it leaning against a stall.
Next morning an old farmer found it there and, as no
one claimed it, he took it home to his wife.

Now *we* know – but the farmer and his wife didn't,
of course – that this was a magic umbrella. If you held
it open in your hand and counted three, you found
yourself at home. If you counted five, you found
yourself where you most wanted to be at that
moment. If you counted *seven*, there you were floating round and round the top of the nearest church
steeple!

When next the farmer's wife went to market, she
took the magic umbrella with her because it was
raining. As she sat at her stall in the afternoon with
the umbrella open in her hand, a boy came up and
asked if she had any eggs left. 'Why, yes,' said the old
lady, 'just three. Hold out your basket,' and she
counted the eggs into it. ONE-TWO-THREE.
Whee-ee-ee – there she was in her own kitchen, the
umbrella still open in her hand.

'Ee-ee, Mother,' said her daughter in astonishment, 'I never saw you come in. How did you get here?'

'I don't rightly know, dearie,' said the poor old lady. 'Make me a cup of tea, will you, love. I feel quite out of breath, I don't know why.'

So she sat down and drank a cup of tea and soon felt quite all right again.

A few days after she went to see her married daughter and, as the sun was shining, she took the magic umbrella with her as a sunshade. After they had washed up after dinner, she and her daughter went to sit by a busy road to watch the cars go by. The farmer's wife was very interested in cars. It was a treat for her to watch them, so she sat down on the grass verge and opened her umbrella to shield her from the sun.

'Eh, what a power of cars there do be to be sure,' she said. 'ONE-TWO-THREE-FOUR-FIVE – I wish I were in one of 'em, I do!'

Whee-ee-ee! There she was, sitting in one of the cars on an old lady's lap. The old lady screamed, and her husband stopped the car at the side of the road and said indignantly, 'How dare you jump into my car like that! Get out at once!'

The farmer's wife scrambled out quite bewildered and stood in the middle of the road with the cars streaking by. Her daughter came hurrying up and said, 'Ee-ee, Mother! Whatever made you do that?'

'I don't know, dearie,' said the poor old lady, 'I really don't. I think I must be ill. I'd better go to the doctor tomorrow.'

So the next day she and her daughter went to the doctor and, as it was raining, she took the magic umbrella with her. The doctor felt her pulse – *so* – and looked at her tongue – *so* – and said, 'Oh, yes, you've got a touch of Thingumbobitis. You must take these pink pills three times a day, this green medicine five times a day and these blue pills *seven* times a day. Whatever you do, don't let your nose get cold – it would be most dangerous!'

The poor old lady felt quite confused. As she went out of the surgery she said to her daughter, 'Oh dear! I shall never remember all that. What did he say – blue pills three times a day, yellow medicine five times a day, pink pills – how many times had I to take those? ONE-TWO-THREE-FOUR-FIVE-SIX-SEVEN . . .'

Whee-ee-ee! There she was, floating round and round the church steeple, her umbrella open in her hand like a parachute.

Well – her daughter looked up in amazement. 'Ee-ee!' she said. 'I've never seen my mother do that afore!'

Off she went to the fire station for help and along came the fire engine at full gallop. One by one the firemen set up their long ladders until they reached almost to the top of the steeple. Then, while everyone

watched in suspense, a fat fireman climbed up and up until he could just reach the old lady's skirts – she was still floating round and round the church steeple. Down, down, down he came, tugging her with him. But just when she was *so* high above the ground, a sudden gust of wind caught the umbrella and blew it away out of sight and the old lady fell to the ground with a bump.

'Ee-ee, Mother!' said her daughter. 'Whatever made you go up there? I've never seen you do that afore!'

'Eh, I don't know – ' said the poor old lady. 'I think I must be really ill. I'd better go to bed.'

And so she did. She stayed there for two whole weeks and she was never ill in that way again. BUT – if *you* should find an umbrella which doesn't belong to you, be careful. You don't want to find yourself floating round and round the church steeple, do you!

Teddy Robinson Goes to the Toyshop

JOAN G. ROBINSON

Teddy Robinson was a nice, big, comfortable, friendly teddy bear. He had light brown fur and kind brown eyes, and he belonged to a little girl called Deborah. He was Deborah's favourite teddy bear, and Deborah was Teddy Robinson's favourite little girl, so they got on very well together, and wherever one of them went the other one usually went too.

One story about Teddy Robinson and Deborah tells how they went with Mummy to a toyshop. After looking at all the dolls Mummy said:

'I don't think it's much use our looking at dolls any more. They're all so dear.'

'Yes,' said Deborah, 'and I've just thought what I really would like to buy. Couldn't I have one of those dolls that are really hot-water bottles?'

'Why, yes,' said Mummy. 'What a good idea!'

So they all went along to the chemist's department, and there they saw three different kinds of hot-water-bottle dolls. There was a hot-water-bottle clown, and a hot-water-bottle Red-Riding-Hood, and a hot-water-bottle dog, bright blue with a pink bow.

Deborah picked up the blue dog.

'That's the one I want,' she said. 'Look, Teddy Robinson – do you like him?'

'Isn't he rather flat?' said Teddy Robinson.

'Yes, but he won't be when he's filled,' said Deborah. 'He's a dear – isn't he, Mummy?'

'Yes,' said Mummy, 'he really is.'

'Everybody in this shop seems to be dear except me,' said Teddy Robinson to himself. And he felt grumpy and sad; but nobody noticed him, because they were so busy looking at the blue dog, and paying for him, and watching him being put into a brown-paper bag.

All the way home Teddy Robinson went on feeling grumpy and sad. He thought about the blue-dog hot-water bottle, who seemed to be coming home with them.

'Deborah and Mummy called *him* a dear, too. But I don't think he's a dear. I don't like him at all, and I hope he'll stay always inside that brown-paper bag.'

But when they got home the blue dog was taken out of his brown-paper bag straight away. And when bed-time came something even worse happened. Teddy Robinson and Deborah got into bed as usual, and what should they find but the blue dog already there, lying right in the middle of the bed, and smiling up at them both, just as if he belonged there!

'*Look* at who's in our bed!' said Teddy Robinson to Deborah. 'Make him get out.'

'Of course he's in our bed,' said Deborah. 'That's what we bought him for, to keep us warm. Isn't he a dear?'

Teddy Robinson didn't say a word, he felt so cross. Deborah put her ear against his furry tummy.

'You're not *growling*, are you?' she said.

'Yes, I are!' shouted Teddy Robinson.

'But why?'

'Because I don't like not being dear,' said Teddy Robinson. 'And if I aren't dear why do people always call me "Dear Teddy Robinson" when they write to me?'

'But you *are* dear,' said Deborah.

'No, I aren't,' said Teddy Robinson; 'and now I don't even *feel* dear any more. I just feel growly and grunty.' And he told her all about what he had been thinking ever since they left the toyshop.

'But this is only a hot-water bottle,' said Deborah. 'You are my very dear Teddy Robinson, and you're quite the dearest person in the whole world to me (not counting Daddy and Mummy and grown-ups, I mean).'

Teddy Robinson began to feel much better.

'Push the blue dog down by your feet, then,' he said. 'There isn't room for him up here.'

So Deborah pushed the blue dog down, and Teddy Robinson cuddled beside her and thought how lucky he was not to be just a hot-water bottle.

Soon the blue dog made the bed so warm and cosy that Deborah fell asleep and Teddy Robinson began to get drowsy. He said, 'Dear me, dear me,' to himself, over and over again; and after a while he began to feel as if he loved everybody in the whole world. And soon his 'Dear me's' turned into a sleepy little song which went like this:

> Dear me,
> dear me,
> how nice to be
> as dear
> a bear
> as dear old me.
> Dear you,
> dear him,
> dear them,
> dear we,
> dear *every* one,
> and dear,
> > > dear
> > > me.

And then he fell fast asleep.

And that is the end of the story about how Teddy Robinson went to the toyshop.

Teddy Robinson Is a Polar Bear

One day Teddy Robinson sat under the apple-tree looking at a picture book. A little wind rustled the branches over his head, and soon one or two leaves came fluttering down around him.

'Dear me,' said Teddy Robinson, looking upward, 'this tree seems to be wearing out. Its leaves are falling off.'

Then the wind blew a little stronger and one or two pages blew out of the book (which was an old one) and fluttered away on to the grass.

'There now,' said Teddy Robinson, looking after them, 'this book seems to be wearing out too. It's losing its leaves as well.'

The wind blew stronger still, rustling the leaves and bending the long grass sideways.

'Br-r-r-r!' said Teddy Robinson, 'it's cold. The wind's blowing right through my fur.'

'It's getting thin,' said a sparrow, flying past. 'You should have chosen feathers like me. They wear better.'

'Good gracious, do you mean I'm wearing out too?' said Teddy Robinson. But the sparrow had gone.

The garden tortoise came creeping slowly past.

'I'm quite worn out myself,' he said. 'I've been tramping round and round looking for a nice warm place to go down under. This pile of leaves looks as good as anywhere. Are you coming down under too, teddy bear? Winter's coming soon and the nights will

be growing cold.'

'Oh no,' said Teddy Robinson, 'I always have a nice warm place down under Deborah's blankets when it's cold at nights.'

'Oh well, here goes,' said the tortoise, and he began burrowing, nose first, deep into the pile of leaves.

'Anyway,' said Teddy Robinson to himself as he watched the tortoise disappear, 'I wouldn't care to spend the winter down there. Besides, I can't quite remember what it is, but I believe there's something rather nice happens in winter-time. Something worth staying up for.'

So the tortoise stayed buried, and the wind blew colder, and more and more leaves fell off the apple-tree. And because it had grown too cold to play in the garden any more, Teddy Robinson and Deborah played indoors or went for walks instead.

Then one day Teddy Robinson looked out very early in the morning, and saw that all the garden was white with snow. There was snow on the trees, and snow on the roofs of the houses, and thick snowflakes were falling in front of the window. He pressed his nose against the glass and stared out.

'Goodness gracious me,' he said, 'someone's emptied a whole lot of white stuff all over our garden. How different it looks!'

A robin flew down from a near-by tree, scattering snow as he flapped his wings. He hopped on to the windowsill and looked at Teddy Robinson through the window with his head on one side.

'Good morning!' he chirped. 'What do you think of this? Got any crumbs?'

Teddy Robinson nodded at him behind the glass and said, 'Good morning. I'm afraid I haven't any crumbs just now, but I'll ask Deborah at breakfast-time. What's it like out there?'

'Lovely,' said the robin, puffing out his red waistcoat. 'But you wouldn't like it. Snow is all right for white polar bears, but not for brown indoor bears. Well, I must be off now. Don't forget my crumbs!'

He flew away, and Teddy Robinson went on watching the snowflakes falling outside the window and sang to himself:

> There's snow in the garden,
> and snow in the air,
> and the world's as white
> as a polar bear.

When Deborah woke up, Teddy Robinson showed her the snow as proudly as if he had arranged it all himself (it felt like his snow because he had seen it first), and she was very pleased. As soon as breakfast was over she put out a saucer full of crumbs on the sill (because he had told her about the robin), and then she put on her coat and boots.

'I'm going to be very busy now,' she said. 'Andrew and I are going to dig away all the snow from people's gates.'

'Can I come?' said Teddy Robinson.

Deborah looked out. 'Yes,' she said, 'it's stopped snowing snow. You can sit on the gate-post and watch us.'

So Deborah and Andrew started clearing the snow away from all the front gates while Teddy Robinson sat on his own gate-post and watched them. And after a while it began to snow again. Teddy Robinson got quite excited when he saw the big snowflakes settling on his arms and legs, and he began singing again, happily:

> There's snow in the garden,
> and snow in the air,
> and the world's as white
> as a polar bear.
>
> Snow on the rooftop,
> and snow on the tree,
> and now while I'm singing
> it's snowing on me!

'Hooray, hooray,' he said to himself. 'Perhaps if it snows on me long enough I shall be all white too. I should love to be a polar bear.'

And it did. It snowed and snowed until Teddy Robinson was quite white all over, with only his eyes and the very tip of his nose showing through.

'I don't believe even Deborah would know me now,' he said, chuckling to himself. And it seemed as if he was right, because when Deborah came running back for dinner Teddy Robinson kept quite still and didn't say a word, and she ran right past him into the house without recognizing him.

'This *is* fun!' said Teddy Robinson. 'All this snow must be the nice thing I'd forgotten about, that happens in winter-time. It was worth staying up for.' And he felt sorry for the poor old tortoise who was down at the bottom of the pile of leaves and missing it all.

How surprised Deborah will be when she comes

back and finds I've turned into a polar bear, he thought.

But Deborah didn't come back, because after dinner she made a snowman in the back garden and forgot all about him. Teddy Robinson didn't know this, but he was having such a jolly time being a polar bear all by himself on top of the gate-post that he didn't notice what a long time she was.

First the Next Door Kitten came picking her way along the wall, shaking her paws at every step. She looked at Teddy Robinson as if she didn't quite believe in him, and they had a little conversation.

'Who are you?'
'I'm a polar bear.'
'Why aren't you at the North Pole?'
'I came to visit friends here.'
'Oh!'
Then Toby the dog (who belonged to Deborah's friend Caroline) came galloping up. He was a rough

and noisy dog who liked chasing cats and barking at teddy bears. The Next Door Kitten jumped quickly over the wall into her own garden, but Teddy Robinson kept quite still until Toby was sniffing round the gate-post. Then he let out a long, low growl.

Toby jumped and barked loudly. Teddy Robinson growled again.

'Who's that?' barked Toby.

'Gr-r-r, a polar bear. Run like mad before I catch you!'

Toby looked round quickly, but couldn't see anyone.

'Go on, *run*,' said Teddy Robinson in his big polar bear's voice, 'RUN!'

Toby didn't wait for any more. With a yelp which sounded more like Help! he ran off up the road as fast as he could go.

'Well, I'll never be frightened of *him* again,' said Teddy Robinson.

Then the robin flew down from the hedge and perched on the gate-post beside him and cocked a bright eye at him.

'Hallo,' he chirped. 'Who are you?'

'I'm a polar bear.'

The robin looked at him sideways, hopped round to his other side, and looked again. Then Teddy Robinson sneezed.

'You're not,' said the robin. 'You're the brown bear who lives in the house. I saw you this morning. I told you then this snow isn't right for an indoor bear like you. You'll catch cold. But thanks for my crumbs. I'll look for some more at tea-time. I hope you'll be having toast? I like toast.' And before Teddy Robinson could answer he had flown off again over the white roofs of the houses.

It grew very quiet in the road. People's footsteps made no sound in the snow and it seemed as if the world was wrapped in cotton wool. Teddy Robinson was beginning to feel cold. Soon one or two lights went on in the houses, and in a window opposite he could see a lady getting tea ready.

'I wonder if she is making toast,' he said to himself, and felt a little colder.

Then he began thinking about the tortoise tucked away in the big pile of leaves.

'He must be quite cosy down there,' he said, and he thought of the leaves all warm and crunchy and smelling of toast, and almost wished he had gone down too.

'But of course, if I had, I should never have been able to be a polar bear sitting on a gate-post,' he said; and to keep his spirits up he began singing a polar bear song:

> Ice
> is nice,
> and so
> is snow.
> Ice
> is nice
> when cold winds blow –

but the words were so cold that they made him sneeze again.

'Never mind,' said Teddy Robinson bravely, 'I'll think of something else. I'll make up a little song called The Polar Bear on the Gate-Post.'

But it was hard to find anything to rhyme with gate-post, and the more he thought about it, the more he found himself saying 'plate' instead of 'gate', and 'toast' instead of 'post', so in the end, instead of singing about a Polar Bear on a Gate-Post, he was singing about an Indoor Bear on a Plate of Toast, which wasn't what he'd meant at all.

'But it *would* be nice and warm sitting on a plate of toast,' he said to himself. And then suddenly he thought, Of course! *That's* the nice thing that happens in winter-time. It's not snow at all. It's toast for tea!

And at that moment the robin came flying back chirping, 'Toast for tea! Toast for tea! Is it ready?'

When he found the saucer empty on the window-sill and poor Teddy Robinson still sitting in the snow, with an icicle on the end of his nose, the robin was quite worried.

'They must have forgotten about you,' he said. 'I'll remind them.' And he flew up to the window and beat his wings hard on the glass. Then he flew back to Teddy Robinson.

Deborah came to the window and looked out.

'Oh, Mummy!' she called. 'There's the robin, and he's sitting on – he's sitting on – why, it's Teddy *Robinson*, all covered in snow and looking just like a polar bear! And the robin's sitting on his head.'

'Oh, don't they look pretty!' said Mummy. 'Just like a Christmas card.'

Then Teddy Robinson was brought in and made a great fuss of. And afterwards, while Mummy made the toast for tea and Deborah put out fresh crumbs for the robin, he sat in front of the fire and bubbled

and mumbled and simmered and sang, just like a
kettle when it's coming up to the boil:

> Tea and toast,
> toast and tea,
> the tea for you
> and the toast for me.
> How nice to be a warm, brown bear
> toasting in a fireside chair.

When bedtime came Teddy Robinson's fur was still
not quite dry, so Mummy said he had better stay
downstairs and she would bring him up later. So
Deborah went off to bed, and Mummy went off to
cook grown-up supper, and Teddy Robinson toasted
and dozed in the firelight and was very cosy indeed.

Then Daddy came home, puffing and blowing on
his fingers and stamping the snow off his shoes. He
took a little parcel out of the pocket of his big
overcoat and gave it to Mummy. Inside was a fairy
doll, very small and pretty, with a white-and-silver
dress, and a silver crown and wand.

'Oh, a new fairy for the Christmas-tree!' said
Mummy, standing her upon the table. 'How pretty!
That is just what we need. Now come and have
supper, it's all ready.'

So Daddy and Mummy went off to their supper,
leaving the fairy doll on the table and Teddy
Robinson in front of the fire.

'A new fairy for the Christmas-tree,' said Teddy
Robinson to himself. 'The *Christmas*-tree. I'd forgotten all about it,' and his fur began to tingle. He
suddenly remembered how the Christmas-tree
looked, with toys and tinsel all over it, and little

coloured lights, and a pile of exciting little parcels all round it. And he remembered himself, sitting close beside it in his best purple dress, trying to see if any of the parcels were for him, without looking as if he was looking. And then he remembered how there always was a parcel for him, and how it was always just what he wanted.

'Of course!' he said. '*That's* the nice thing that happens in winter-time, that I'd forgotten about. It's not snow (though that's very nice), and it's not toast for tea (though that's nicer still), but it's Christmas, and that's nicest of all!'

There was a rustling over his head and the fairy doll whispered in a tiny little voice, 'Would you like a wish, teddy bear? If you like you can have one now. It will be the very first wish I've ever given anyone.'

Teddy Robinson said, 'Thank you,' then he thought hard, then he sighed happily.

'It seems a terrible waste of a wish,' he said, 'but I don't think I've anything left to wish for. I'll wish you and every one else a very merry Christmas.'

And that is the end of the story about how Teddy Robinson was a Polar Bear.